CLICK, CLACK, MOO
Cows That Type

20th Anniversary Edition

For my Dad —D.C.
To Sue Dooley —B.L.

ARTIST'S NOTE:

For this book I did brush drawings using Windsor Newton lamp black watercolor on tracing paper. I then had the drawings photocopied onto one-ply strathmore kid finish watercolor paper and applied watercolor washes to the black drawings. The advantage to this method is that I can get as many copies on the watercolor paper as I want, and I can experiment with the color, choosing the finishes that I like the best.

ATHENEUM BOOKS FOR YOUNG READERS • An imprint of Simon & Schuster Children's Publishing Division • 1230 Avenue of the Americas, New York, New York 10020 • Text copyright © 2000 by Doreen Cronin • Illustrations copyright © 2000 by Betsy Lewin • Jacket illustrations (underside) copyright © 2002, 2004, 2006, 2015, 2016, 2018, 2020 by Betsy Lewin • All rights reserved, including the right of reproduction in whole or in part in any form. • ATHENEUM BOOKS FOR YOUNG READERS is a registered trademark of Simon & Schuster, Inc. Atheneum logo is a trademark of Simon & Schuster, Inc. • For information about special discounts for bulk purchases, please contact Simon & Schuster Special Sales at 1-866-506-1949 or business@simonandschuster.com. • The Simon & Schuster Speakers Bureau can bring authors to your live event. For more information or to book an event, contact the Simon & Schuster Speakers Bureau at 1-866-248-3049 or visit our website at www.simonspeakers.com. • Book design by Anahid Hamparin • The text for this book was set in 30 point Filosofia Bold. • Manufactured in China • 0320 SCP • This Atheneum Books for Young Readers anniversary edition June 2020 • 10 9 8 7 6 5 4 3 2 1 • CIP data for this book is available from the Library of Congress. • ISBN 978-1-5344-6302-8 • ISBN 978-1-4424-6051-5 (eBook)

CLICK, CLACK, MOO
Cows That Type

by Doreen Cronin   pictures by Betsy Lewin

Atheneum Books for Young Readers
New York London Toronto Sydney New Delhi

Farmer Brown has a problem.
His cows like to type.
All day long he hears

Click, clack, **moo.**
  Click, clack, **moo.**
Clickety, clack, **moo.**

At first, he couldn't believe his ears.
Cows that type?
Impossible!

Click, clack, **moo.**
Click, clack, **moo.**
Clickety, clack, **moo.**

Then, he couldn't believe his eyes.

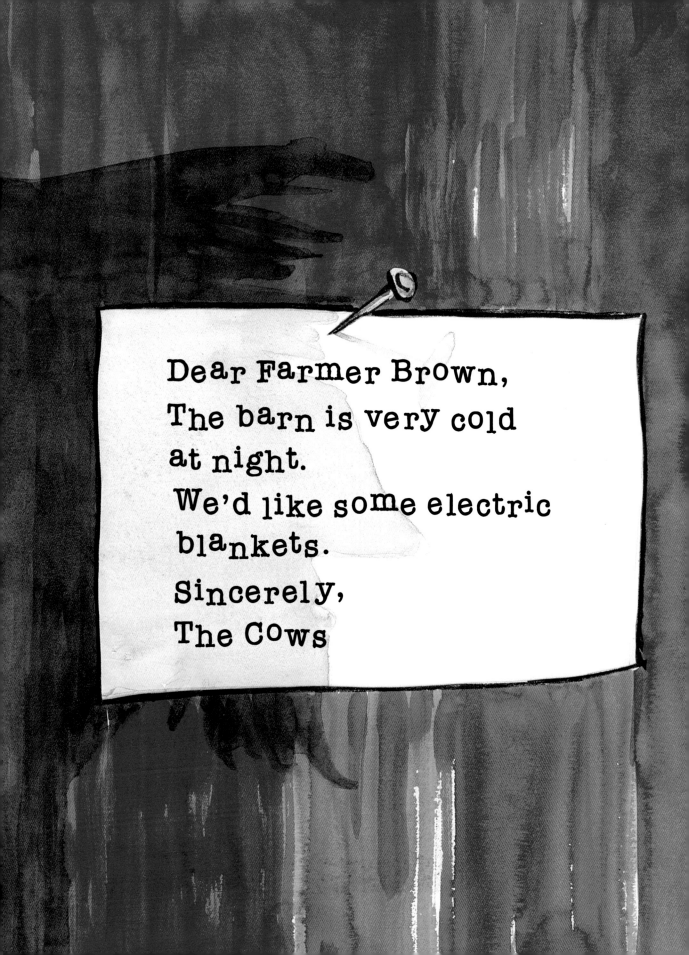

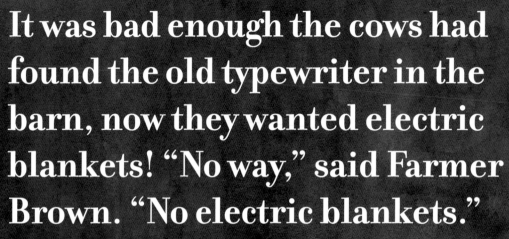

It was bad enough the cows had found the old typewriter in the barn, now they wanted electric blankets! "No way," said Farmer Brown. "No electric blankets."

So the cows went on strike. They left a note on the barn door.

"No milk today!" cried Farmer Brown. In the background, he heard the cows busy at work:

Click, clack, **moo.**
Click, clack, **moo.**
Clickety, clack, **moo.**

The next day, he got another note:

Dear Farmer Brown,
The hens are cold too.
They'd like electric
blankets.
Sincerely,
The Cows

The cows were growing impatient with the farmer. They left a new note on the barn door.

"No eggs!" cried Farmer Brown.
In the background he heard
them.

Click, clack, **moo.**
  Click, clack, **moo.**
Clickety, clack, **moo.**

"Cows that type. Hens on strike! Whoever heard of such a thing? How can I run a farm with no milk and no eggs!" Farmer Brown was furious.

Farmer Brown got out his own typewriter.

Dear Cows and Hens:
There will be no electric blankets.
You are cows and hens.
I demand milk and eggs.
Sincerely,
Farmer Brown

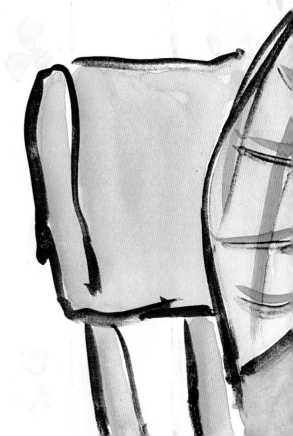

Duck was a neutral party, so he brought the ultimatum to the cows.

The cows held an emergency meeting. All the animals gathered around the barn to snoop, but none of them could understand Moo.

All night long, Farmer Brown waited for an answer.

Duck knocked on the door early the next morning. He handed Farmer Brown a note:

Dear Farmer Brown,
We will exchange our typewriter
for electric blankets.
Leave them outside the barn door
and we will send Duck over
with the typewriter.
Sincerely,
The Cows

Farmer Brown decided this was a good deal. He left the blankets

next to the barn door and waited for Duck to come with the typewriter.

The next morning he got a note:

Dear Farmer Brown,
The pond is quite boring.
We'd like a diving board.
Sincerely,
The Ducks

Click, clack, **quack.**
 Click, clack, **quack.**
Clickety, clack, **quack.**